LORD SHIVA

AN ULTIMATE ADIYOGI

DAKSH . P . ACHARYA

Contents

CHAPTER ONE

Shiva's Birth

Shiva is also referred to as *Swayambhu* (meaning 'self-existing') because he was not born from the womb of a woman. There is an interesting story behind the birth of Lord Shiva.

One day, Brahma and Vishnu were arguing about each other's predominance and importance in the universe. As the debate was on, a mysterious pillar appeared in front of them. Both of them could not understand what the pillar was and wondered if there exists any other supreme power than them. They decided to unravel the mystery of the mighty pillar. Lord Brahma transformed into a goose and flew upward to find the apex of the pillar while Lord Vishnu transformed into a boar and dug the ground to find the root.

However, they could find neither and came back to the place from where they started only to witness the emergence of Lord Shiva from the pillar. It made them accept the fact that Lord Shiva was the supreme power.

CHAPTER TWO

The God of Transformation

Lord Shiva is a part of Trinity of Brahma, Vishnu, Mahesh and is associated with Moksha which is relief from the cycle of birth and death.

By Moksha, He is actually taking us out from the illusionary world of Kama, Krodha, Moha, Mada and Lobha and making us realize who we are and what is our true purpose of existence. Thus the power of destruction of Lord Shiva has a great purifying power on a universal level. The destruction opens the path for a new creation of the universe, a new opportunity for the beauty and drama of universal illusion to unfold. Being Satyam, Shivam and Sundaram which denotes the Truth, Goodness and Beauty, Lord Shiva represents the essence of impeccable goodness and godliness. Shivaratri puja performed on the Festival called Maha Shivratri invites the blessings of Lord Shiva and His divine consort, Goddess Parvati.

His favorite ornament is Rudraksha which He wears on his arms, wrists, neck, waist and hair mat. He holds a snake coiled around His neck, a Trishul, drum and Kamdalu in hand and wears a tiger skin. His body is smeared with ash.

In Hindu mythology there are various forms of meditations and different paths for yogis but Shiva represents the art of meditation in its most absolute form. In meditation, not only mind is made still but everything is dropped. In deep meditation or Samadhi, even the object of the meditation (like a mantra, Tantra or Yantra) is transformed into its formless essence, which is the essence of absoluteness and "Purna"(completeness). Thus Shiva stands for letting go everything in the world of forms. The path of Lord Shiva is undoubtedly the path of the ascetic yogi.

All Avtars (Forms) of Lord Shiva

Shiva has different forms: The first being Aghora (which resides in the cremation grounds), then Ishana (most often appears as the Shivalingam), the third being "Tat Purusha" where He is meditating, then Varna Deva (the eternally auspicious Shiva) and then Sadyojat or Braddha Rudra (the old wrathful form). The last also forms of the Lord has the deepest connection to the Rudrakshas and Rudrakshas mala - a rosary made of the dried fruits of the Rudraksha tree.

Yet another form is the Nataraj, where the Lord Shiva Nataraj's dance implies both the destruction and the creation of the universe and reveals the cycles of death, birth and rebirth. His Dance of Bliss is for the welfare of the world. In the pose of Nataraj, the King of Dance is giving darshan to his beloved devotees within the "Hall of Consciousness", which is the heart of the human. Under his feet, Shiva crushes the demon of ignorance called Apasmara Purusha, caused by forgetfulness. One hand is stretched across his chest and points towards the uplifted foot, indicating the release from earthly bondage of the devotee. The fire represents the final destruction of creation, but the dance of the Nataraj is also an act of creation, which arouses dormant energies and scatters the ashes of the universe in a pattern that will be the design of the ensuing creation.

Then in His Mahamrityunyaya form, Lord Shiva is depicted as the great conqueror of death and giver of immortality. The Mahamrityunjaya mantra is one of the two main mantras of the Vedas, next to the Gayatri mantra. It is chanted to eradicate death and disease.

Another main form of Shiva is Ardhnarishwara, half Shiva, half Shakti.

CHAPTER THREE

The Story of Nandi

Once there was virtuous sage by the name Shilada, who did not have any children of his own. He decided to worship Lord Shiva to get a special child blessed by him. He prayed intensely and immersed himself in austerity for thousands of years.

Pleased by his dedication, Lord Shiva finally appeared before Shilada. He said "Wake up dear Shilada and tell me what boon do you seek?"

"My dear Lord, I have only one aspiration. I wish to have a child", replied Shilada.

Shiva smiled and said "You shall have it soon", before vanishing from the place.

Shilada returned home as a happy man, knowing that the Lord would bless him with a very good child. The next day he went to the farm to begin his ploughing, when he found a beautiful baby in the field before his plough. The baby was bright as sun. Shilada stared at the baby transfixed, when he heard a voice from the heaven, "SHILADA, TAKE THE CHILD. BRING HIM UP WELL!"

Shilada was overjoyed as he took the boy home. He named the boy Nandi. Right from his childhood, Nandi was devoted to Lord Shiva. Shilada brought up the child with love and care. . He taught his son the Vedas, the arts of the medicine, fighting, dancing, singing and several other sacred texts. Nandi was a brilliant boy and learnt everything very fast. Shilada felt very proud of the child.

Some years later, two sages , Mitra and Varuna came to Shilada's home. "Welcome great sages!" Shilada gave the rishis some refreshments, "Please sit and make yourself comfortable,, Shilada offered them his home for rest. "Nandi!" Shilada called his son. Nandi came from inside the house. "Nandi please make sure these sages are well looked after."Nandi smiled and nodded his head saying, "Yes father!"

Nandi looked after the two sages well and after staying there for couple of days, the sages said its time to leave as they have to continue their journey. Before they leave, Shilada and Nandi both sought their blessings.

Mitra and Varuna first blessed Shilada, "Have a long and happy life, Shilada. You have made us very happy.

When Nandi fell at the feet, the two sages looked slightly sad. Slowly they said, "Be well son! Be good to your parents and teachers!" And they walked off.However Shilada noticed the change in the expression of the sages. He ran outside the house, "Great Rishis! he said breathlessly. He turned around and made sure that Nandi was inside the house and could not hear him, and asked the sages, "You looked sad while blessing my son!" "Is something wrong?"Mitra looked at Shilada with pity, "I cannot wish your son a long life...."

Shilada was crestfallen. He asked "What is going to happen to my son?"

"Your son, does not..." Varuna cleared his throat, "...does not have long to live, Shilada. I am sorry to bring this news to you, but that his fate." He said lamely, looking at the horrified expression on Shilada, face.

Shilada stood there transfixed for a long time. After a long time, he slowly walked back home with stooping shoulders and a broken heart.

Nandi immediately guessed something was wrong, "What is it Father? What happened?" Nandi asked, vigorously shaking his father.

Slowly and painfully, Shilada narrated his conversation with the two sages.

He expected Nandi to be scared or even that Nandi would even start crying. However Shilada was surprised when he saw Nandi is laughing. "You were scared of what the sages said!"

Shilada wondered what could be so funny and looked at his son without any expression.

"Father, you have told me that you have seen Lord Shiva..." Nandi said with great devotion in his eyes. "Anybody who has seen Lord Shiva cannot be afraid of what the sages just said." "Father, if it, my fate to die, then Lord Shiva, can reverse my fate!,He is the most powerful God and can do anything. Do you think he would let anything happen to us, when we worship him?" Nandi looked at his father. "I don't think so father." Nandi said softly.

Shilada looked at his son as if looking at him for the first time. Slowly Shilada nodded his head and smiled.

Nandi bowed to his father. "Bless me father!"

Shilada blessed his son, "Be victorious my son!"

Nandi then went near the River Bhuvana. He entered the river and began his penance. His devotion was so great and his concentration was so high, that Lord Shiva appeared in front of him.

"Nandi, open your eyes!" said the three eyed God tenderly, looking at Nandi.

Nandi opened his eyes and before his eyes stood the most beautiful person he had seen in his whole life. Nandi looked at the God wanting to savour his image. He felt that he had nothing more left to ask. Instantly a thought came to his mind, if only I could always stay with the Lord.

Shiva looked at Nandi, "Nandi, you penance was so powerful that it dragged me here! Ask me anything I will grant it to you!" Shiva said.

"Lord I wish to be with you always." The words were out of Nandi,mouth before he could stop them.

Shiva smiled. "Nandi I have just lost my bull, on which I used to travel. Henceforth Nandi, you shall have a face of a bull. You shall stay in my home at Kailash. You shall be the head of all my Ganas and you will be my companion, my vehicle and my friend, always!"

Nandi closed his eyes as tears flowed through them. The Lord had granted him his wish and a lot more.Since then Nandi became Shiva's vehicle, doorman, his companion and the head of all of Shiva's attendants , the Ganas.

Thus by sheer devotion Nandi was not only able to overcome his fate, he also rewrote it.

Shiva, Parvati & Ganesha

Shiva's wife was Parvati, often incarnated as Kali and Durga. She was in fact a reincarnation of Sati (or Dakshayani), the daughter of the god Daksha. Daksha did not approve of Sati's marriage to Shiva and even went further and held a special sacrificial ceremony to all the gods except Shiva. Outraged at this slight, Sati threw herself on the sacrificial fire. Shiva reacted to this tragedy by creating two demons (Virabhadra and Rudrakali) from his hair who wreaked havoc on the ceremony and beheaded Daksha. The other gods appealed to Shiva to end the violence and, complying, he brought Daksha back to life but with the head of a ram (or goat). Sati was eventually reincarnated as Parvati in her next life and she re-married Shiva.

" SHIVA IS THE DESTROYER WHO ENDS THE CYCLE OF TIME WHICH, IN TURN, BEGINS A NEW CREATION,,

With Parvati, Shiva had a son, the god Ganesha. The boy was in fact created out of earth and clay to keep her company and protect her while Shiva went on his meditative wanderings. However, Shiva returned one day and, finding the boy guarding the room where Parvati was bathing, he enquired who he was. Not believing the boy was his son, and thinking him an impudent beggar, Shiva called up the bhutaganas demons who fought the boy and eventually managed to distract him with the appearance of the beautiful Maya and, whilst he admired the beauty, they lopped off his head. At the commotion, Parvati rushed from her bath and screamed that her son had been killed. Realising his error, Shiva then sent for a new head with which to make the boy whole again but the nearest at hand was of an elephant. And so Ganesha, the elephant-headed god, was born. Other sons of Shiva are Skanda or Karttikeya, the god of war and Kuvera, the god of treasures.

Ganga (the goddess who personified the river Ganges) was given to Shiva by Vishnu who could not take any more of the constant quarrels between his then three wives of Lakshmi (goddess of good fortune), Saraswati (goddess of wisdom) and Ganga. To cushion Ganga's fall to the earth, and prevent such a great river destroying civilisation, Shiva caught her in his hair topknot; once again, illustrating his quality of self-sacrifice.

" SHIVA NATARAJA IS THE LORD OF THE DANCE WHO SWEEPS AWAY ILLUSION & IGNORANCE.,,

CHAPTER FIVE

Shiva in Mythology

As with any major god, Shiva was involved in many adventurous episodes which illustrate his virtuous character and offer instruction on how to live correctly. For example, self-sacrifice is emphasised when Vasuki, the king of Serpents, threatened to vomit snake venom across the seas. Shiva, assuming the form of a giant tortoise or turtle, collected the venom in his palm and drank it. The poison burned his throat and left a permanent blue scar, hence one of his many titles became Nilakantha or Blue Throat.

Another celebrated episode describes how Shiva became associated with the bull Nandi. One day, Surabhi, who was the original mother of all the world's cows, began to give birth to an untold number of perfectly white cows. The milk from all these cows flooded the home of Shiva, somewhere in the Himalaya. Angry at this disturbance to his meditation, the god struck the cows with fire from his third eye. In consequence, patches of the cows' hides were turned brown. Still angry, the other gods sought to calm Shiva down by offering him a magnificent bull - Nandi, the son of Surabhi and Kasyapa - which Shiva accepted and rode. Nandi also became the protector of all animals.

Shiva is closely associated with the Linga (or Lingham) - a phallus or symbol of fertility or divine energy found in temples to the god. Following the <u>death</u> of Sarti, and before her reincarnation, Shiva was in mourning and went to the Daru forest to live with *rishis* or sages. However, the wives of the *rishis* soon began to take an interest in Shiva. In jealousy, the *rishis* first sent a large antelope and then a gigantic tiger against the god but Shiva swiftly dealt with them and wore the tiger skin thereafter. The sages then cursed Shiva's manhood which, in consequence, fell off. When the phallus struck the ground, earthquakes began and the *ricsis* became afraid and asked for forgiveness. This was given but Shiva told them to forever after worship the phallus as the symbolic Linga.

CHAPTER SIX

Shiva in Art

In Asian art Shiva may be represented in slightly different ways depending on the particular culture: Indian, Cambodian, Javanese etc. but he is most commonly depicted naked, with multiple arms and with his hair tied up in a topknot. He often has three horizontal stripes and a third vertical eye on his forehead. He wears a headdress with a crescent moon and a skull (representing the fifth head of Brahma, which he decapitated as punishment for the god lusting after his own daughter Sandhya), a necklace of heads, and snakes as bracelets. In this guise, he usually represents Nataraja and performs the Tandava cosmic dance within a circle of fire which represents the never-ending cycle of time. He holds the divine fire (agni) which destroys the universe and the drum (damaru) which makes the first sounds of the creation. One hand makes the calming abhayamudra gesture and another points to his left foot, symbol of salvation. He also stamps one foot on the dwarf figure Apasmara Purusha who represents illusion and who leads men away from the truth.

Shiva may also be depicted standing on one leg with the right leg folded in front of the left knee and holding a rosary in his right hand, the typical posture of ascetic meditation. Sometimes he also rides his white bull, carries a silver bow (Pinaka), holds an antelope, and wears a tiger or elephant skin, all symbolic of his famed prowess as a hunter.

Hanuman, devotee of Lord Rama and son of Anjana ad Kesari, is believed to be the eleventh incarnation of Lord Shiva. It is said that the radiance of all celestials came in the form of Shiva's radiance from which Hanuman was born.

Kamadeva, the Hindu god of love and desire, could not distract Lord Shiva. When Indra and other gods were waging war against demon Tarakasura, they approached Shiva for help. Since the demon can only be defeated by Shiva's son but Shiva was busy meditating. The devas then asked Kamadeva to break Shiva's meditation. The love god enters Shiva abode in the form of breeze and awakens Shiva with a flower arrow. This angers Shiva and he turns Kamadeva into ashes.

As per Hindu mythology, Lord Shiva along with one crore gods and goddesses were visiting Kashi. He asked them to take a night's rest in Unakoti, Tripura and wake up before the sunrise the next day. Since none of them were able to wake up on time Shiva cursed them to become stone images.

There are many legends associated with tandava, one of which says, the demon Apasmara challenged Shiva. Shiva took the form of Nataraja to suppress Apasmara – the symbol of ignorance. He accepted the challenge and took the form of Nataraja to perform tandava. During the performance, Shiva crushed Apasmara under his right foot. Since Apasmara cannot die to maintain the balance between knowledge and ignorance, Shiva remained in his Nataraja form. This avatar of Shiva gives the message that ignorance can be overcome by knowledge, music and dance.

CHAPTER SEVEN

Lord Shiva and the fisherwoman

Lord Shiva starts explaining the Vedas to his wife Parvati, and that goes on for several years. But one day, Parvati loses her concentration. The annoyed Shiva curses her to go to the earth and take birth as a fisherwoman.

Parvati takes birth as a baby girl and the chief of fishermen community, Parvaras, takes her to his home. He names her Parvati and brings her up.

Meanwhile, Shiva realizes his mistake and starts missing his wife. Seeing this, his disciple Nandi suggests Shiva call Parvati back. Shiva replies that he can't do it because as per her birth, she is destined to marry an angler.

Hearing this, Nandi comes up with a plan to reunite Shiva and Parvati. He takes the form of a big shark and goes into the sea where the fishermen go fishing. He starts troubling the fishermen. Knowing about it, Parvaras announces that whoever catches the whale would get to marry his daughter.

The chief and his daughter Parvati pray to Lord Shiva to help them. Listening to Parvati's prayers, Lord Shiva turns into a young fisherman and comes to the fishermen's rescue. Nandi happily lets his master catch him. This way, Shiva remarries Parvati.

CHAPTER EIGHT

Lord Shiva and Bhasmasura

In the Himalayas, there was a rakshasa named Bhasmasura, who spent years meditating to please Lord Shiva. Appeased by his devotion, Shiva appears before him and asks him to make a wish.

The clever Bhasmasura asks, "Lord, grant me the boon that whatever I touch with my right hand will turn into ashes immediately." Shiva grants the boon not realizing the evil intentions of the rakshasa.

Bhasmasura intends to test the boon on the lord himself, to turn Shiva into ash and gain the supreme power. Even as he chases Shiva, Lord Vishnu witnesses this and decides to save Shiva from the rakshasa.

Vishnu turns into a beautiful woman named Mohini and appears before Bhasmasura. Her mesmerizing beauty makes him fall for her and propose her. Mohini tells him that she would marry him if he can dance like her and defeat her.

Bhasmasura agrees and follows every step of Mohini with élan. As his confidence keeps increasing, Mohini does a step by putting her right hand on her head. The over-confident rakshasa forgets about his boon and puts his right hand on his head. Immediately, he turns into ash.

CHAPTER NINE

Lord Shiva and the halahala poison

Do you know how Lord Shiva got the name 'Neelkanth'? There is a <u>fascinating story</u> behind it.

Sage Durvasa once curses all the gods, leaving them powerless and depriving them of all the fortunes. The gods seek help from Lord Vishnu, who suggest them to churn the ocean to retrieve nectar that can help them become immortal and bring back the lost fortunes.

The gods partner with the demons to combine their strengths for churning the ocean. Vasuki, the serpent, is made the churning rope and mount Mandara as the churning rod. During the churning process, many things come out of the ocean including the *halahala* poison, which had the capability to wipe out the entire creation in the universe.

Terrified with the spread of the poison, all the gods approach Lord Vishnu again. He directs them to Lord Shiva, as he is the only one who can protect them. Lord Shiva offers to drink the poison but squeezes his throat tight to prevent the poison from entering the body.

The poison turns Shiva's throat blue and hence he is also called Neelkanth, wherein *neel* means 'blue' and *kanth* means 'throat'

CHAPTER TEN

The story of Sudarshana Chakra

One day, all gods approach Lord Vishnu pleading with him to save them from the attack of the rakshasas. Lord Vishnu says that he does not have enough power to fight the demons and would have to seek Lord Shiva's help. When he reaches Kailash, he finds Lord Shiva in a deep trance. Unwilling to disturb him, Lord Vishnu decides to pray for Shiva until he comes out of his trance.

Vishnu would chant the name of Shiva a thousand times every day by offering one lotus flower against each chant. This goes on for many years before Shiva comes out of the trance one day. Not knowing that Shiva has come out of his trance, Vishnu continues his chanting for the day.

Shiva decides to play a trick on Vishnu, and secretly removes one lotus from the bunch that Vishnu had arranged. After Vishnu chants for 999 times, he realizes that one flower is missing from his collection. He immediately plucks out his eye and offers it at the feet of the Shiva.

Impressed by Vishnu's devotion, Shiva tells him to ask for a boon. Vishnu asks him to give the power to defeat the demons to save all the gods. Lord Shiva gives him a round disc, called the 'Sudarshana Chakra', which has the power to kill anything.

CHAPTER ELEVEN

Ravana shakes mount Kailash

Ravana is a great devotee of Lord Shiva. But one day he tries to pull down the abode of Lord Shiva, the mount Kailash. Though he fails in his attempt, this act angers Shiva and he traps Ravana below the mount Kailash.

Then, Ravana starts singing songs in praise of Shiva. He cuts one of his heads to make a veena (an Indian musical instrument) and uses the tendons as strings to play music. This goes on for several years before Shiva is impressed. He forgives Ravana and sets him free.

CHAPTER TWELVE

Lord Shiva's third eye

Lord Shiva is also called 'Trilochan' as he has three eyes. There is an interesting story behind the third eye of Lord Shiva.

One day when Shiva was meditating, his consort, Parvati thought of playing a game with him. She came from behind and closed his eyes with both her hands. It is believed that the right eye of Shiva represents the sun and the left eye represents the moon.

Closing his eyes led to chaos everywhere as the universe sunk into darkness. Immediately, Shiva created the third eye on his forehead with his divine powers to emit fire. Also, the heat from the fire caused Parvati's hands to perspire. The sweat, combined with the powers of both Lord Shiva and Goddess Parvati, transformed into their child named Andhaka.

CHAPTER THIRTEEN

Why does Shiva cover his body with ash?

One day the powerful sage Parnada was cutting some grass when he cut his finger out of which the sap of a tree oozed out instead of blood which filled him with pride. Shiva witnessed this and took the disguise of an old man and asked the safe the reason for his delight for which Parnada replied that he had become the most pious man in the world. To this the old man (Shiva) questioned his joy saying it was just sap; when trees and plants are burned down they turn into ash. He then demonstrated it by slicing his finger and spilled ash. Sage then realized that it is Shiva before him and his forgiveness for his ignorance.

CHAPTER FOURTEEN

Story of 12 Jyotirlings

The first time Lord Shiva manifested himself as a Jyotirlinga was in the night of Aridra Nakshatra. The first Jyotirlinga is the very popular **Somnath** that is in the state of Gujarat. It was destroyed and re built about sixteen times. This is so case in the olden days it was considered to be the richest temple in India. Studded with gold and gems it was indeed the most sorted temple in India. The story goes like this. Chandra (moon) married all the twenty seven daughters of Daksha. Nevertheless, he loved only Rohini. He gave all importance to her while the other daughters of Daksha were lonely and upset. This made Daksha very upset and he wanted to ensure that Chandra spends quality time with his other wives too. Chandra never gave any heed to this and kept spending time with Rohini alone. Daksha one day lost his temper and cursed Chandra. He said that Chandra will lose all his light. Chandra immediately became lightless as a result the whole world became dark. All the gods met and decided that they should request Daksha to forgive Chandra. After a lot of request from the gods Daksha said that Chandra will have to start worshiping lord Shiva and when lord Shiva gives him his light he will start shining again. Chandra immediately reached Prabas and started to worship the lord Shiva. Soon he was blessed and lord appeared. He gave him the light and moon started to shine again. It is believed that even today on moonless night Chandra comes and dips in the holy water of the sea here and starts shining again. This is how lord Shiva also got the name of Someshwar.

The second Jyotirlinga in the list is **Mallika Arjuna Swamy temple** that is located in Andhra Pradesh. The story goes like this. Shiva and Parvati were not able to decide which son of theirs should get married first. So they told them to go around the world. The one who would be able to do this first will get married first. Lord Kartik took his peacock and started the trip but Ganesh decided to go round his parents and said this was his world. Shiva and Parvati were very pleased at this so they got him married to Riddhi and Siddhi the daughters of Viswaroopan. Lord Kartik on his return got to know what happened. He was very ashamed of himself and said he will never get married. He went to the mount Kravunja and started living there. Shiva and Parvati when got to know this they decided to visit their son. Lord Shiva visited on a no moon day and Parvati on a full moon day. This is exactly where this temple is.

The third Jyotirlinga is the very popular <u>Mahakaleshwar jyotirlinga</u> in Ujjain. It is a very sacred place and is situated on the bank of Rudra sagar. This part of the country was once ruled by a king named Chandrasena. He used to worship lord Shiva. The people would also regularly worship the lord. One day the kingdom was attacked by king Ripudamana who had a demon with him named Dushan. This demon got a unique ability it could become invisible. The kingdom was shattered and all the people started to pray to Lord Shiva. Lord appeared and protected the city. The people of Ujjain requested him to stay there itself and protect them. Shiva could not say and he decided to stay in Ujjain and take care of his devotees. It is belived that the lord still lives there.

The fourth Jyotirlinga in India that has been worshiped for ages is the very famous <u>Omkareshwar jyotirlinga</u> in the state of Madhya Pradesh. There are many stories that revolve around this shrine. However, it is belived that Lord Shiva had appeared here to defeat the danavas on request of the gods. Some say he had appeared here on request of mount Vindya and blessed him that he would become a mighty mountain unless he stops affecting lord Shiva's followers. Some say that king mandhata used to worship lord Shiva here. The lord was so pleased with him that he decided to live here.

Another Jyotirlinga (fifth) of prime importance is the <u>Kedarnath jyotirlinga</u> which is located in the beautiful state Uttarkahand. It is mostly closed in winters as no one can go there. Pandavas wanted to get rid of their sins so that they could go to Swarg. However, they were told that they could do so only if they could see lord Shiva and be blessed by him. So they started their search. After a long search they finally saw lord Shiva at this spot where the Jyotirlinga is today. The lord said that he will stay in this place in the form of a triangular shaped Jyotirlinga. This is one of the most popular Jyotirlinga in India and is also a holy place. Every year a huge number of devotees visit this temple.

<u>Bheemshankarjyotirlinga</u> is the sixth Jyotirlinga that we are going to discuss about. It is located near Pune in Maharashtra. The temple is old and has an interesting story to it too. In this area lived an Asura named Bhima. When he grew a little old he was told by his mother karkati that Kumbhakaran the brother of King Ravana was his father. His mother also told him that his father was killed by lord Vishnu in one of his incarnations (lord Rama). Bhima decided he will avenge the death of his father. He started to pray Lord Brahma and was granted immense powers by the lord. Bhima as expected misused his powers and started havoc. He would kill innocent people. He would torture saints and even kill children. He once took Kamarupeshwar a big Shiva devotee as captive. The lord got very upset at this. The anger even increased when Bhima told Kamarupeshwar to worship him and not the lord Shiva. Kamarupeshwar denied this and as a result Bhima raised his sword to kill him. This is when lord Shiva came to the rescue of his devotee and he killed Bhima. All the gods requested the lord Shiva to stay in this place and so he manifested himself as the Bheemshankar Jyotirlinga.

The <u>Kashi Vishwanath</u>is another very famous nslation means ruler of the universe. The city is the oldest in the world and has a three thousand fife hundred year old history. It is said that this city can never be destroyed. It is a place where Brahma, Vishnu and Mahesh live at the same time. Anyone can attain Moksha here. There is no sin on earth that cannot be washed here. Every year a huge number of people visit this place. It is said that lord Shiva himself had made this city.

Another very popular Jyotirlinga (eighth) that is situated in the state of Maharashtra is the famous <u>Trimbakeshwar jyotirlinga</u>. There are three lingas here signify Brahma, Vishnu and Mahesh. There is a crown that is bejewelled with gems that is used to cover these lingas. It is now days kept from four to five in the evening only on Monday. The use of water is eroding the actual Jyotirlingam. That is why it is covered and kept with a metal shield. The legends say that Gautam rishi used to live here with his wife Ahilya. Gautam Rishi was blessed by lord Shiva with a bottomless pit from where he could get any amount of grain and food. The other Rishi's got very jealous of Gautam Rishi. They decided to send a cow there and killed it. Gautam Rishi got very upset with this and he prayed to lord Shiva that he wants Ganges to flow in this part of the country so that his sins are washed off. Lord Shiva granted his wish. The lord decided to stay here by the name of Trimbakeshwar. It is said that it can full fill all desires.

Now we move on to the ninth Jyotirlinga that is called <u>Baidyanath jyotrilinga</u> in Jharkhand. This Jyotirlinga has a very interesting story to it. <u>Ravana the lord of Lanka</u> was a huge devotee of lord Shiva. He once felt that if Shiva does not reside in Lanka then Lanka can be destroyed. He wanted to make Lanka invincible. Lord Shiva agreed to his prayers and gave him a lingam. He warned him that if he places the lingam in any part of earth before he reached Lanka it will get fixed to that land and no one will be able to remove it. Ravana started his journey back from Kailash. On the way it was evening and he had to do his evening prayer. However, he could not do it with the Jyotirlinga in his hand. He saw a shepherd boy and requested him to hold the Jyotirlinga and also warned him not to place it down. The boy agreed but warned him that if there is a delay from him he will place it and go. Ravana said he will be back soon. The shepherd boy was actually lord Ganesh and he was there at the request of the gods. When there was a delay from Ravana, lord Ganesha kept the Jyotirlinga on the ground and he left. When Ravana saw this he became very upset but in spite of trying very hard he could not remove it. Since then it is present in this part of the country. It is one of the very popular Jyotirlinga.

The next or tenth Jyotirlinga that we are going to discuss is the <u>Nageshwar Jyotirlinga</u>that is located near Dwarka in Gujarat. It is said that there was a Shiva devotee named Supriya who lived in this area. She was once attacked and captivated by Daaruka. When she started to call lord Shiva he appeared and he killed Daaruka. After this he started to live here as <u>Nageshwar Jyotirlingam</u>.

The eleventh Jyotirlinga that we must mention here is<u>Rameshwar jyotirlinga</u>in Tamil Nadu. It is one of the <u>Char Dham</u>. There are two lingams here. One was brought by Hanuman from Kailash and the other by Sita Devi. The Vishwalingam is worshiped first as it was brought by Hanumana. The one brought by Sita is worshiped second. The same is done even today. This is exactly the place where lord Rama worshiped lord Shiva after he defeated Ravana. It is also known for its unique architecture. It has the largest hallway as compared to any other temple in India. It was built over years. It is considered to be a hugely sacred place by the Hindus. Many visit this place every year.

The last of the 12 Jyotirlinga that we are going to discuss is the <u>Grishneshwar jyotirlinga</u>in Maharashtra. It is located very close to the Ajanta and Ellora caves in Aurangabad. Many years ago a woman named Kusuma used to live here. She would worship the lord. Her ritual she would immerse the shiv linga in a tank and then worship it. The villagers would respect her a lot and come to her for advice. Her husband's other wives were very jealous of her so they killed her son in cold blood. After her son's death too she continued the rituals. One day while she immersed the shiv linga in the tank. Lord Shiva appeared along with her son. The villagers were surprised to see this. Since then it is said that lord Shiva resides here. It is also known as Kusumeshwar Jyotirling

Shiva Lingam

The Shiva Lingam is rounded , elliptical iconic image set on a circular base or Peetham or the parashakthi , the manifesting power of the god. The lingas are usually made up of stone some of which are carved accordingly while the others are naturally existing called the Svayambhu and gets shaped by a swift flowing river. Some lingas can also be made of metal, precious stones, gems, wood or transitory material like ice. Some literature believe that the transitory Shiva linga can be made from 12 different materials like from sand, rice, cooked food, river clay, cow dung, butter, rudraksha seeds, ashes, sandalwood, darbha grass, a flower garland or molasses. The supreme lord does not have any form and in fact every form is his form. Just like how when we see smoke we know that there is fire , the very moment we see a Shiva lingam we can visualise the presence of the ultimate and supreme lord.

CHAPTER SIXTEEN

Myths about Shiva Lingam

However the common myth exists between people that the Shiva lingam depicts the male genital organ. However this is absolutely misleading and baseless and such irrelevant misinterpretation was done during the later part of the vedic period when the Indian literature came into the hands of the foreign scholars. Thus Shiva lingam is just a differentiating mark and certainly not a sex mark. According to the Linga Purana which states that:

प्रधान पुरकृतरि यदाहुरुलगिउत्तम ।
गध-वरण-रसहनि शब्द-सपरशादविरजति ॥

According to that it means that the lingam is devoid of colour, taste , hearing or touch and is considered as prakriti or nature.

Another very popular belief among the people is that they consider lord Shiva as a destructor only. However the nature itself is a lingam or symbol of the lord. The Shiva lingam is a clear mark of Shiva who is the creator , sustainer and the destructor.

Another quote from the Skanda Purana depicts that the whole universe is created from the supreme Shiva and it finally gets submerged there.

आकाश लगिमतियाहुः पृथ्वी तस्य पीठिका।
आलयः सर्व देवाना लयनारुलगिमुच्यते ॥
(स्कन्द पुराण)

This means that the endless sky is the linga and the earth is the base. And at the end of it all the entire universe and all the gods finally merge into the Linga from where it originated.

CHAPTER SEVENTEEN

Significance of Shiva Lingam

The Linga denotes the ascending powerful and radiating energy of consciousness and life in our nature. This energy can be seen in the mountain, the thundercloud, the trees and even in human beings. In fact the most important Shiva site in the Himalayas at the Kedarnath are rocks in the shape of small mountains. There are 12 Jyotirlingas or in other words the light forms of Shiva at 12 special temples throughout the world which is extremely well known and popular. The great enlightened sage Ramana Maharshi who stayed in the Himachals is said to be the place for fire linga of the supreme lord. The state of Tamil Nadu has lingas for the five elements mainly for earth, water, fire, air and ether at special temples in the region known as Panchabhoota Sthalam.

Just like how lord Shiva himself is considered to be pure light in its primal undifferentiated state called the Prakasha Matra , even the Shiva linga is described most often in terms of light transparent and crystal like. The linga is often considered as the pillar of light and hope. According to the Vedic rituals, they believed that fire could be made to rise in the shape of a pillar and eventually take the shape of a man. Dharma refers to something that upholds things and the Shiva linga is the universal pillar of dharma. This pillar is an inner symbol demonstrating the erect spine and the concentrated mind. With regards to the human nature there is the force of the Prana linga or the pillar which upholds the physical body to the currents that emanate from it and is thus called so. Then the deeper intelligence which provides us the power of insight to discriminate the right and wrong is called the Buddhi Linga and lastly the Atma linga is the ultimate or the determinative force of our nature that always remains steady and elevated throughout our lives and is termed as the Atma linga.

In addition the Linga and the yoni which is the standing stone and the ring base always go hand in hand . This also depicts the union of the male and female energies or the shiva and shakti principles. They also believe that the linga and yoni are united like the chakra or the wheel with the linga as the axis and the yoni as the circumference. In fact each chakra depicts the union of the Shiva Shakti energies at its particular level of manifestation with the Shiva energy running upward through the spine and the Shakti energy is the horizontal current forming the various lotuses of the chakra. Both these forces are essential to create a dynamic motion.

While practicing yoga the divine experience of the Shiva linga can create a pillar of light, energy, peace and eternity and helps to expand the mind and bring deep peace and steadiness to the heart and the soul. Even the waves of Shakthi that radiate can help us acquire grace, love and wisdom. It has been proved that the linga is one the best ways of meditation and to calm the mind and be in touch with our inner being and go way beyond all the materialistic needs, agitations and sorrows of the world. However according to the Ayurvedic treatment, they believe that the creation of the Prana linga allows deep healing and rejuvenation. The Vedic science considers the Shiva linga as the power of light behind the sun, moon , planets and the stars. In accordance with the Vastu shastra, the Shiva linga is the spiritual and the vital energy in the house that stabilizes everything.

The two common forms of the Shiva lingam are the Chala or the moveable form and the Achala or the fixed form.

Chala lingam is the one which is usually kept in the shrine at one home or is prepared temporarily with materials like sand, clay, dough and is often dispensed after the worship. Some consider that the lingas worn on the body in the form of pendent as Chala lingam and is usually made up of mercury,metals or quartz. The Achala or the fixed lingam are the ones that are installed in temples and are not moveable. There are certain rules which need to be obeyed for the Achala lingams like they need to be offered prayers at fixed time without being failed even once and complete sanctity must be maintained. They are usually made up of black stone.

The Shiva lingams that are usually made up of quartz have unique and special significance. Such lingas do not have a colour of their own but they tend to take up the colour of the object that comes in contact with it. The indescribable power of the Shiva linga is that it can induce concentration of the mind by just looking at it and that is exactly why ancient scholars and sages preferred the worship of Shiva lingam and its installation in the temples. It is believed that listen to the message of the Shiva lingam and it will say" i am one without a second".

The worship of the Shiva linga has become an extremely popular form of worship especially among the Hindus. In fact every city, town ,village will atleast have one temple with a Shiva linga . According to the Purana there are 12 Jyotirlingas in various parts of the India and they are at <u>Somnath in Gujarat</u>, <u>Mallikarjun Jyotirlinga in Srisailam</u>, <u>Kashi Vishwanath</u> (UP), <u>Trimbakeshwar Shiva Temple</u> (near Nasik, Maharashtra), <u>Mahakaleshwar</u> (MP), <u>Omkareshwar Jyotirlinga</u> (MP), <u>Kedarnath</u> (Himalaya), <u>Baidyanath Dham</u> (Jharkand), <u>Rameshwaram Temple</u> (Tamil Nadu), <u>Nageshwar Jyotirlinga</u>, <u>Bhimashankar Temple</u>, <u>Grishneshwar Jyotirlinga</u>. Similarly there are <u>Panchabhoota lingams</u> which represents the 5 elements and they are located in Kalahastisvar, Jambukcsvar, Ekambaresvar, Natraja, Arujachalesvar.

CHAPTER EIGHTEEN

Puja of Shiva Lingam

It is considered that the Shiva linga helps to connect the devotee with the supreme lord. The Linga puja helps in better understanding of the lord. Since the lord is formless and we still say that he is without a beginning and an end it might be difficult for a devotee to understand. And hence lord Shiva appeared in the form of Jyothirlinga before Brahma and Vishnu and thus is a pure symbol of the lord.

It is extremely important to be pure and hence the devotee needs to take a bath and wear clean washed clothes before commencing the puja. Hymns praising the lord are chanted to create a mood of worship followed by blowing the conch or ringing bells after sitting in front of the lingam and thus denoting the beginning of the puja. . The Panchamrit abhishekam is done where in five holy liquids is poured over the lingam which can include either water from the river Ganges, honey, sugarcane juice, milk, yogurt, ghee, seawater, coconut water, milk, fragnanat oils, rose water. Usually only milk of cow is used for the puja. While pouring the liquid <u>Om Namah Shivaya</u> is chanted repeatedly while others chant the lords name 108 or 1008 times. This is followed by cleaning the linga with the water from the ganges and is then smeared with sandalwood paste and is decorated with flowers. It is believed that water and sandalwood paste helps to keep the lingam cool as lord Shiva is always in a highly inflammable state. In some temples it is noticed that a cooling liquid is placed above the lingam and water constantly trickles down from it. Sweets, fruits, coconuts are offered to the lord followed by lighting of the camphor and the aarti is commenced. Ringing of the bells and blowing the conch marks the end of the puja. White ash is rubbed on the forehead of the linga and it is distributed among the devotees.

CHAPTER NINETEEN

Ardhnareshwar

Ardhanarishvara is a composite androgynous form of Shiva and his consort Parvati. This form is shown as a fusion of half-male and half-female forms, split down in the center. The right half is depicted as Shiva, while the left half shows the female form of Parvati.

The very name Ardhanarishvara implies "the Lord who is half-woman". This form of Shiva is also referred to as Ardhanarisha, Ardhanarinateshwara, Ardhayuvateeshwara, Ardhagaureeshwara, Gaureeshwara, Naranaari, Parangada and Ammiappan.

Since Ardhanarishvara represents the perfect synthesis of male and female forms, it also embodies the Prakriti and the Purusha, the feminine and masculine energies of the cosmos and also illustrates how Shakti, the Sacred Feminine, is inseparable from Shiva, the male principle of God. This form also symbolizes the all-pervasive, all-enduring nature of Lord Shiva.

CHAPTER TWENTY

Origin of Ardhanarishvara

The origin of the concept of Ardhanarishvara can be traced back to hermaphrodite figures in both the ancient Hindu and Greek cultures. The earliest images of Ardhanarishvara date back to the Kushan era, records of which exist from the first century CE.

It is believed that the iconography of Ardhanarishvara developed and evolved during the Gupta period. The concept of Ardhanarishvara continues to be a popular iconographic form and can be found in most Shiva temples throughout India. But strangely, there are very few temples in this country that are actually dedicated to this deity.

It is believed that the early iconography of Ardhnarshvara could have been inspired by the Vedic literature's composite figure of Yama-Yami, the combination of the primordial Creator Vishwaroopa or Prajapati and Agni, the Fire God. This figure appears as a bull, who is also a cow. Interestingly, the androgynous forms of Hermaphrodites and Ageists are famous in Greek mythology as well.

The <u>Brihadaranyaka Upanishad</u> says that this androgynous form occurs as a result of Purusha splitting himself into two parts, male and female. These two halves copulate, thereby producing all life. The Shwetashwatara Upanishad also talks about Rudra, the antecedent of the Puranic Shiva, the maker of all and the root of Purusha and Prakriti (the female principle), adhering to Samkhya philosophy.

As is the case with Hindu mythology, there are several legends related to the emergence of the Ardhanarishvara concept. The earliest legends originated in the Puranic canons. This half male-half female form also finds mention in the Mahabharata epic.

According to the Skanda Purana, Goddess Parvati asks Shiva to permit her to stay with him forever, embracing him "limb-to-limb". Ardhanarishvara was thus formed.

The Matsya Purana relates that Brahma, pleased with Parvati by her penance to him, rewards her with a flawless golden complexion. This makes her many times more attractive to Shiva, who fuses into her to form the Ardhanarishvara.

There is also another story relating to this form. It is said that the demon Andhaka wanted to make Parvati his wife. Vishnu rescued Parvati and brought her to his own abode. But the demon refused to relent and followed her there as well. Parvati then revealed her Ardhanarishvara form to him, seeing which the demon lost interest in her and left. The interesting thing about this story is that Lord Vishnu was amazed to see this form as well and also saw himself in the female part of the form.

In the Kalika Purana, Parvati suspects Shiva of infidelity, when she sees her own reflection in Shiva's breast. An argument ensues between them, which is also resolved as quickly. Thereafter, Parvati wishes to stay eternally with Shiva, fusing with him as one single body.

Yet another lore talks about Parvati's jealousy when she sees Ganga perched on Shiva's head. Though Shiva tries to appease her by placing her on his lap, Parvati continues to be upset. This is when Shiva unites with the Goddess in the form of Ardhanarishvara.

According to the Shiva Purana, Brahma or Prajapati, the creator of all male beings, was once faced with a steep decline in the pace of creation. A flustered Brahma approached Shiva for help. Shiva appeared before him in the form of Ardhanarishvara and Brahma prayed to the female half of Shiva to help him create females in order to continue the process of creation. The goddess then created various female powers from her body, thus speeding up the process of creation.

According to a popular Tamil legend, Goddess Uma (another aspect of Parvati) once playfully closed the eyes of Shiva, thus plunging the entire world into darkness. All living beings on earth suffered due to this eternal darkness. Uma, realizing her folly, was forced to leave Kailas and started to worship the Linga in order to absolve herself of her sin and to reunite with her Lord. Lord Vishnu then appeared before her and gave her instructions on the austerities she needed to perform in order to attain her Lord once more. Uma commenced her penance accordingly. At this time, the evil demon, Mahishasura, came to the fore and started disturbing those of earth. This is when Uma takes the form of Devi Durga and engages in a long battle with him, finally slaying him. Lord Shiva then manifests as the Fire on top of the hill. He then merges into the Devi and gives darshan as the Ardhanarishvara, with the Devi as his left half. This is celebrated by devotees as the Deepa vali day and the Lord Ardhanarishvaramoorthy blesses his devotees in his Jyoti Swarupa (form of Light).

According to various other Puranas such as the Vishnu Purana, Vaayu Purana, Linga Purana, Kurma Purana, Skanda Purana and Markandeya Purana, Rudra, an aspect of Shiva, emerges from Brahma's forehead. So hot is Rudra that he burns Brahma in the process. Brahma asks him to divide himself and the latter agrees to do so, thus giving rise to several hundreds of beings, including the 11 Rudras and many, many female Shaktis. The Goddess then reunites with Shiva and promises him that she will be reborn on Earth as Sati and would wed him in human form as well. The Ardhanarishvara form then enjoys his own other half by the "Path of Yoga" and creates both Brahma and Vishnu from her body. It is believed that at the start of each new Yuga or epoch, the Ardhanarishvara is ordained to reappear and continue ahead on the path of bringing forth new creation on this Earth.

The common belief is that Shiva, being the Supreme Lord, split himself into two halves, male and female. Only some schools of Shaktism believe that Shakti split her body into male and female halves.

CHAPTER TWENTY-ONE

When Shiva Lost His Home – The Legend of Badrinath

This is where Shiva and Parvati lived. It is a magnificent place at around 10,000 feet in the Himalayas. One day, Narada went to Narayana or Vishnu and said, "You are a bad example for humanity. All the time you are just lying around on Adishesha, and your wife, Lakshmi, is constantly serving you and spoiling you silly. You are not a good example for other creatures on the planet. For all the other beings in the creation, you must do something more purposeful."

To escape this criticism and also work for his own upliftment, Vishnu came down to the Himalayas looking for the right kind of place to do his sadhana. He found Badrinath, a nice little home, with everything just the way he thought it should be – an ideal place for his sadhana.

He found a house there and went into it. But then he realized this is Shiva's abode – and that man is dangerous. If he gets angry, he is the kind who can cut off his own throat, not just yours. The man is very dangerous.

So, Narayana transformed himself into a little child and sat in front of the house. Shiva and Parvati, who had gone out for a walk, returned home. When they came back, at the entrance of their home a little baby was crying. Looking at this child crying his heart out, Parvati's maternal instincts came up and she wanted to go pick up the child. Shiva stopped her and said, "Don't touch that child." Parvati replied, "How cruel. How can you say that?"

Shiva said, "This is not a good baby. Why does he land up at our doorstep by himself? There is no one around, no footprints of parents in the snow. This is not a child." But Parvati said, "Nothing doing! The mother in me will not allow me to let the child be like this," and she took the baby into the house. The child was very comfortable, sitting on her lap, looking very gleefully at Shiva. Shiva knew the consequence of this but he said, "Okay, let's see what happens."

Parvati comforted and fed the child, left him at home and went with Shiva for a bath in the nearby hot water springs. When they came back, they found the doors were locked from the inside. Parvati was aghast. "Who has closed the door?" Shiva said, "I told you, don't pick up this child. You brought the child into the house and now he has locked the door."

Parvati said, "What shall we do?"

Shiva had two options: one was to burn up everything in front of him. Another was to just find another way and go. So he said, "Let's go somewhere else. Because it's your beloved baby, I cannot touch it."

This is how Shiva lost his own home and Shiva and Parvati became "illegal aliens"! They walked around, looking for an ideal place to live and finally settled down in Kedarnath. Did he not know, you may ask. You know many things, but you still allow them to happen.

CHAPTER TWENTY-TWO

Bilva Leaves – Why Are They Dear to Shiva?

The famous Bilvashtakam extols the virtues of the vilva leaf and Shiva's love for it. Why is the vilva so revered? By common knowledge, we know that the tree has been held sacred for many millennia and offerings made to Shiva are incomplete without vilva leaves. There are many symbolisms attributed to this leaf: the trifoliate leaves or tripatra are believed to represent various trinities – creation, preservation and destruction; or the three gunas or qualities of sattva, rajas and tamas; or the three syllables that make up AUM, the primordial sound that resonates Shiva's essence. The three leaves are also considered to indicate Mahadeva's three eyes, or the trishul, his emblematic weapon..

Why is one leaf more sacred than another? Is it some kind of a prejudice? After all, everything comes from the soil. Both the neem fruit and the mango fruit come from the same soil but they taste very different, isn't it? How one particular life processes the same soil and how another life processes the same soil is different. What is the difference between a worm and an insect, and yourself and another human being? It is all the same stuff but still what we make out of it is different.

When people are on the spiritual path they are constantly looking for support in every possible way because it is unknown terrain. In Indian culture, every little thing that could support you was identified through observation and meditativeness. They did not leave out even flowers, fruits and leaves. Why is the vilva in particular considered sacred? It has always been said that the vilva is dear to Shiva. What does he care? It's not that it is dear to Shiva. When we say it is dear to Shiva, we mean that in some way its reverberance is closest to what we refer to as Shiva.

We identified many things like this and only those things are offered because they become your means to get in touch. When you offer the vilva to Shiva, you are not going to leave the leaf with him. You are supposed to take it with you after it is offered because this particular leaf has the highest capability to absorb that reverberance. If you place it on the linga and take it, it has the ability to retain the reverberation for a long period of time. It stays with you. You can try this: offer the vilva leaf, put it in your chest pocket and walk around, it will make a difference for you in terms of your health, wellbeing, mental state – everything.

There are many materials like this which are recognized sacred tools that people use. This is not about gods, this is about you and your ability to access something.

9 798887 725130